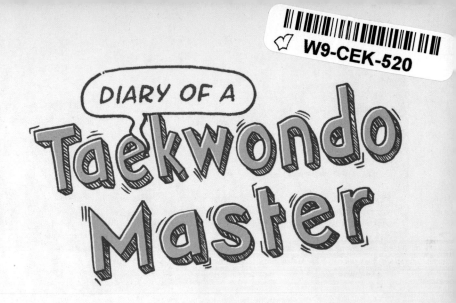

DIARY OF A Taekwondo Master

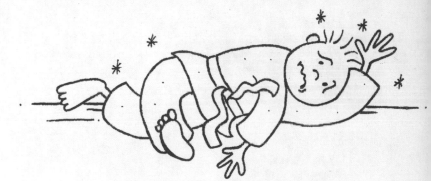

Shamini Flint

Illustrated by Sally Heinrich

ALLEN&UNWIN
SYDNEY · MELBOURNE · AUCKLAND · LONDON

This edition published in 2013

First published in Singapore in 2012 by Sunbear Publishing

Copyright © Text, Shamini Flint 2012
Copyright © Illustrations, Sally Heinrich 2012

Allen & Unwin
83 Alexander Street
Crows Nest NSW 2065
Australia
Phone: (61 2) 8425 0100
Fax: (61 2) 9906 2218
Email: info@allenandunwin.com
Web: www.allenandunwin.com

A Cataloguing-in-Publication entry is available
from the National Library of Australia
www.trove.nla.gov.au

ISBN 978 1 74331 360 2

Text design by Sally Heinrich
Cover design by Jaime Harrison
Set in 10/14 pt Comic Sans

This book was printed in November 2012 at McPherson's Printing Group,
76 Nelson Street, Maryborough, Victoria 3465, Australia.
www.mcphersonsprinting.com.au

10 9 8 7 6 5 4 3 2 1

For Sophia, my beautiful niece

MY TAEKWONDO DIARY

Dad wants me to do taekwondo.

I don't even know what that is!
But knowing Dad, I'm sure
it's dangerous.

Actually, I'm hopeless at art.

(My art teacher, Mrs Quill.)

But I don't care. It will be so wonderful to do something gentle.

For once, I won't get hurt.

Unless someone stabs me with a paintbrush.
And that's unlikely to happen.
I hope.

I'd love to do art, Dad!

You would?

Yes! I'll paint Mum a Christmas present.

(Mum loves anything I do for her, even if it's rubbish – I wish my teachers were like that.)

I bet Spot likes art too. And Fluffy. They could help me!

I'll do my best, Dad! Maybe I'll become quite good! Maybe we can sell my paintings and get rich!

What in the world are you talking about?

Art!

Not art...

...a martial art!

So what does that mean?

My name is Marcus Atkinson. I'm nine years old.
And my dad drives me nuts.

Dad never listens ... but he always REMEMBERS.

Don't believe me? I'll give you examples ...

You see? He never listens
to anything I say.

But he remembers everything I tell him – even though he never listens! How does that work?

Dad, I don't want to do taekwondo!!

It will be great for your self-confidence.

You'll never be shy again...

...even with girls!

Yeah, right.

It will be great for your health.

Yeah, right.

You'll learn self-defence.

No one is trying to attack me, Dad! I don't need self-defence!!

What about that boy you told me about?

Which boy?

JT - the class bully.

You see, he remembers things I tell him – but at the wrong time ...

JT WAS the class bully.

But now we're friends because I rescued his kitten when his dad wanted to send it to the RSPCA.

I'm looking after the kitten (Fluffy) until JT improves his marks and is allowed to have him back.

Dad, JT and I are friends now.

CHAPTER 5

You can never be too careful.

Remember Chapter 5?

Dad's written a book called *Pull Yourself Up by Your Own Bootstraps!*

He's always quoting from it. Did I mention that Dad drives me NUTS?

Anyway, you CAN be too careful ...

Like if you looked right, left, right to cross a road. And then did it again and again and again ... you'd never get across!

Or if you were afraid of closing a door in case you trapped your fingers ... and had to go to the toilet with the door open!

Or if you were too careful about getting a paper cut, so you never opened a book!

But you never open a book. Gemma

Thanks, Gemma.

Gemma is my sister. She enjoys nothing more than sticking post-it notes in my diary with her dumb comments.

I tried to hide my diaries.

In the garden ...

Spot helped her find it.

Under my bed ...

Harriet helped her find it.

In the attic ...

She found it herself.

I give up!

So Dad wants me to learn taekwondo so that I can defend myself against someone who is now my friend.

Great timing, Dad.

Wouldn't it be more useful to teach me to defend myself against ...

Monsters?

Or aliens?

Or ghosts?

Don't be silly, son. There's no such thing as aliens or monsters or ghosts.

What happened to Chapter 5 - you can't be too careful?

Now that JT and I are friends, I don't need taekwondo or self-defence or to become a lean, mean fighting machine.

Dad took me shopping before my first taekwondo class. He bought me some pyjamas.

Maybe taekwondo isn't so bad.
More naps than slaps?
Then we got the armour ...

Shin guards, arm guards, chest guards, helmets and that one guard that is too embarrassing to talk about ...

And the belt – which seemed okay. White.

Just for once, I'd like to try something that doesn't involve wearing body armour. Something safe.

Like skydiving.

Or wrestling bull sharks.

Or messing with Gemma's stuff.

Right, Dad. That was obvious. NOT!

You've got to be kidding me. This guy?

He's smaller than I am. He looks like Yoda from *Star Wars*.

What's he going to teach me?

How to defend myself against rabbits?

Or sheep?

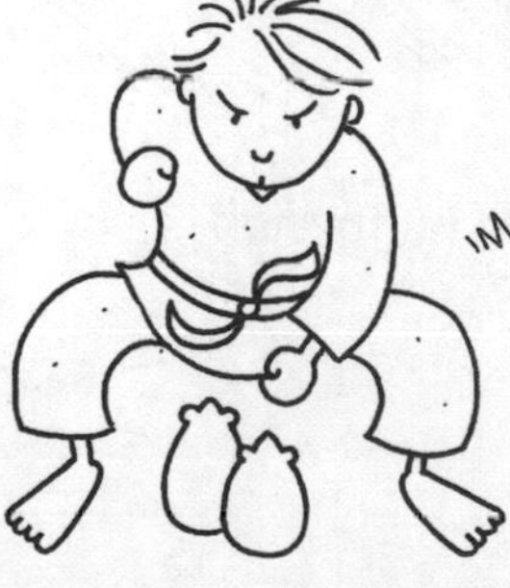

Or hamsters?

I hope for his sake he has a light sabre.

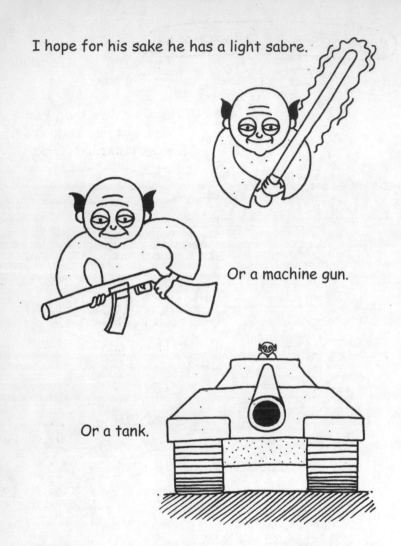

Or a machine gun.

Or a tank.

Otherwise, he's not going to win many fights.
Not even against me.

This guy talks like Yoda as well.

I tried half-a-dozen knots – from bows to reef knots.

Master Choi did not look pleased.

Finally, he waved me over and tied my belt so quickly that I couldn't see what he did.

Now I'll never get it off. Looks like the uniform will be my pyjamas after all.

So, Master Marcus – do you know the way?

The way?

Yes, the way.

Errr – my dad brought me in the car so I'm not sure of the way, I'm afraid.

Master Choi just stared at me.

Do you mean the way to the bathroom? I saw a sign over by the entrance.

Master Choi just stared at me.

The way home? Don't worry about it. My dad will fetch me.

Master Choi just stared at me.

Doesn't he know it's rude to stare?

I was getting desperate. Why was he asking me for directions anyway? This was his dojang!
One of the kids – I think his name is Tom – tried to help me out.

Psssst. 'Do' means the way.

What?

'Do'- you know - taekwon do - means 'the way'.

Ohh!

Errr- no, Master Choi. I do not know the way.

Progress you make, Master Marcus. A cup that is empty may be filled.

Huh?

I'd rather know the way to the ice-cream shop ...

Or the park ...

Or the toy store.

The poomsae you will learn, Master Marcus.

Who's Poom? And what is he saying? And why do I have to learn it?

Turns out the poomsae is a pattern of martial arts steps.

With small steps you can travel great distances.

What about big steps? Won't you travel greater distances with them?

Master Eric will show you the steps.

Master Eric was scary. He had a black belt.
And a black eye.

I showed Eric my moves.

This time I was ...

Master Eric was not amused.

I think he'd have practised some moves on me but Master Yoda, I mean Master Choi, was watching.

Phew!

I guess I won't!

Taekwondo doesn't seem so bad. Boring, but a lot less dangerous than ...

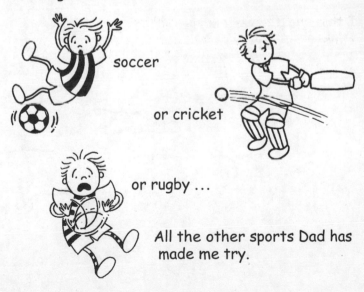

soccer

or cricket

or rugby ...

All the other sports Dad has made me try.

Son, you have to focus.

Taekwondo will help you be prepared for anything!

Really?

So I'll be prepared for ...

A meteor hurtling towards Earth?

Help?

Falling off a boat?

The class play?

Alas ... um ... er ...

Pssst! Alas, poor Yorick ...

Get real, Dad. So far you've bought me a pair of pyjamas that won't come off at bedtime.

But you know Dad – he just doesn't listen ...

I've figured it out now, by the way.
It goes something like this ...

At school the next day ...

He looks scary, but maybe he's a nice guy ...

At recess, I went over to Hulk.

An 'A'? Who'd believe that?

Anyway, I'm not worried.

JT will soon sort this new kid out.

TAEKWONDO LESSON NO. 2

Eric was smiling. He still had his black belt on. But this time he had two black eyes. I didn't even want to think what the other guys looked like.

I did the same.

I shook my head. I needed
to chase the birds away ...

Note to self: Do not annoy Eric.
Or the Hulk.

Dad is worried about me because I don't want to learn to fight.

Him I know. But I'm pretty sure fighting hurts less when you're a plump, animated panda. Apparently the others are martial arts stars. Who knew?

TAEKWONDO LESSON NO. 3

The colour of your belt indicates your level ...

I had to stand in the attention stance for twenty minutes. I didn't mind. Better than giving Eric an excuse to show me a few more blocks.

There was a sudden commotion at the front door.

40

Hulk!
Hulk at taekwondo!!
Hulk in a black belt!!!

Once is bad luck.
Twice is a nightmare, plain and simple.
I doubt there'll be a third time.

At least here Hulk can't ask me to do his homework.

My mum goes to the spa when she needs a massage or to have her nails done.

Marcus, spar with me.

Spa?

I don't think my mum would let me go. But it's very kind of you to ask.

Are you trying to be funny?

He thinks he's funny...

Pssst! Spar means fight.

'No contact' obviously means something different on Hulk's planet than on Earth ...

CHAPTER 3

You have nothing to fear but fear itself.

Really? I can think of lots of things!

How about falling off a boat into a swarm of jellyfish?

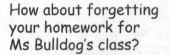

How about forgetting your homework for Ms Bulldog's class?

How about the big guy with the black belt and the bad attitude?

We can talk about it when I stop running!
I'm amazed Dad lived long enough to grow up.

At school the next day, I went looking for JT.

I know JT – he'll let his fists do the talking.

I just hope he hasn't gone soft. He hasn't had much practice recently.

TAEKWONDO LESSON NO. 4

Spot doesn't like taekwondo because he has to wait outside.

I don't like taekwondo because I have to wait inside.

Burrow? Eh? Does he think I'm a mole?

Or an earthworm?

Or a meerkat?

Later Dad told me Master Choi was speaking Korean. Great. That's really helpful. Because I speak Korean. NOT!!!

I didn't say that out loud. I didn't want to spar with Hulk again. Besides, Master Choi probably wouldn't hear me – not if people have been 'kiyooping' at him all these years.

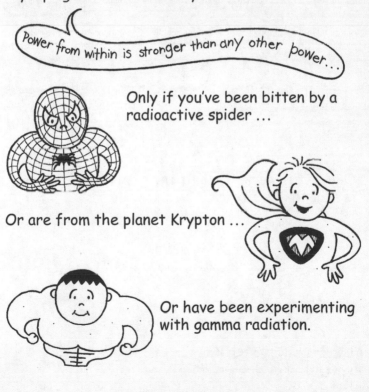

Only if you've been bitten by a radioactive spider ...

Or are from the planet Krypton ...

Or have been experimenting with gamma radiation.

Okay. If it works I might try it on Hulk. His head is shaped like a brick.

Hulk tied me to the lamppost outside after class. Whose bright idea was it to have a belt on this uniform, anyway? Haven't these taekwondo guys ever heard of buttons or a zip?

I had to hang on to Spot. He really wanted to help, but I don't think he should try to bite Hulk. Hulk's sure to taste bad. And he might bite back.

I let Spot and Hulk do the growling.

Spot chewed through my belt.

I walked home.

I was really excited.

JT would soon fix this problem with Hulk.

Hulk would probably learn an important lesson and turn into a really nice guy.

The sort of person ...

Who lets little old ladies have his seat on trains ...

Or finds lost puppies ...

Or rescues kittens from trees.

I can't wait!

JT- we have to meet Hulk behind the gym tomorrow.
You need me to sort him out?
Yes please.
. . . . .
Well...
...I guess I owe you for saving Fluffy...
All right, I'll do it!
Thanks, JT.
Phew!
What a relief.
Chapter 29 - Stand up for yourself!
I don't need to stand up for myself, Dad. I have JT!

You're sure JT can beat Hulk?
G
Of course I'm sure!!
Positively sure!
GULP.
Absolutely definitely positively sure.

I took Fluffy and Spot to visit JT that evening. We drop in often so JT can play with Fluffy.

He was doing his Maths homework when we got there.

Poor JT. It must have been a lot easier for him when he used to make me do his homework.

I waited in the garden with JT's dad. He scares me.

He was gardening. Guess that's not so scary.

It would be tough not to have your pet with you. I hugged Spot. I'd be really upset without him.

No fights?

What about Hulk tomorrow behind the gym?

What if JT's dad finds out?

JT will never get Fluffy back!!

And it will all be my fault!!!

But if JT doesn't turn up, I'm going to spend the rest of my life ...

Doing Hulk's homework ...

Tied to lampposts ...

Afraid of my own shadow ... or his.

So what are you going to do ??
Gemma

I don't know!!!

Any ideas?

Anyone?

HELP!!!

I had nightmares last night.

I dreamt that I was being chased by a sea serpent ...

who looked like Hulk.

I dreamt I was being eaten by a three-headed
monster ...

and all three heads
looked like Hulk.

Worst of all?
I dreamt that Hulk was given a Young Maths Whiz
of the Year award – because of my work!!!

But today I knew what I had to do ...

I explained how JT would never get Fluffy back if he got into a fight at school.

Okay??
OKAY??
Dad was right! Communication is the key to success!!!

Poor JT. I couldn't let that happen. I just couldn't.

Communication is the key to success? Really, Dad?

I'd have more success talking to a brick wall ...

Or a tortoise ...

Or Gemma!

Hey!

At the next taekwondo class, I saw the competition notice.

Hulk doesn't want to fight me?
No.
Phew!
You were afraid of losing?
No-but Dad said if I got in a fight, I'd never get Fluffy back.
Oh...
...but you were still going to do it?
Yeah- can't have you doing his Maths homework for the rest of your life!
Thanks, JT. It was great knowing you...
RIP Marcus
I hear you're gonna take part in the competition?
Yup.
Hulk is going to flatten you...

He's going to chew you up and spit you out...

He's going to turn you into mashed potatoes...

He's going to...

Okay! Enough already! I get it!!

I'm history...

Like the Romans.

Like the Ancient Greeks.

Like the dinosaurs.

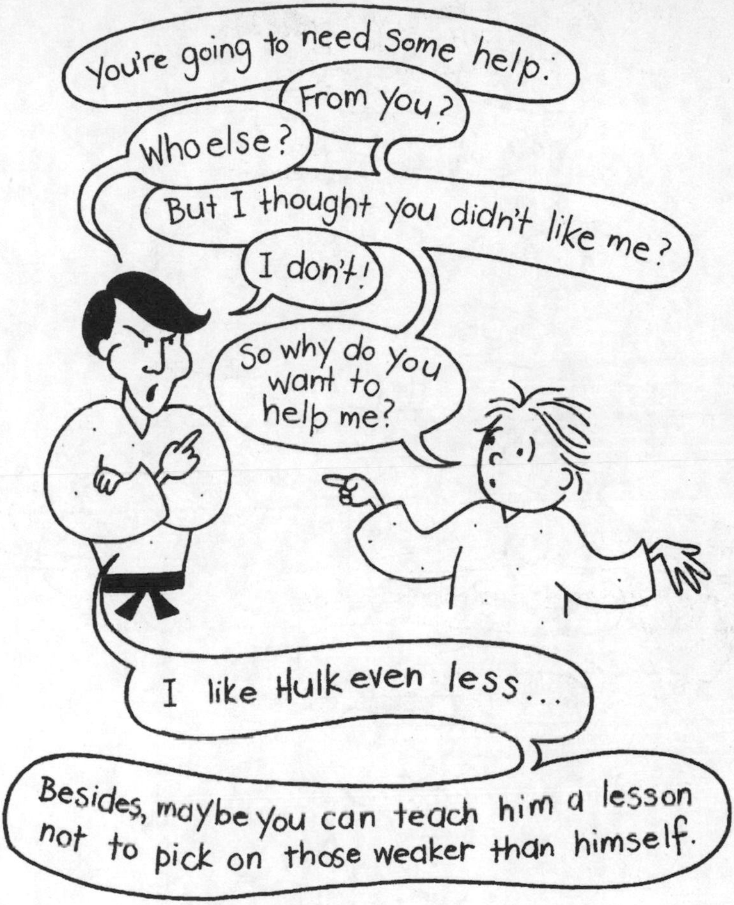

Yeah, right! That's going to happen – NOT!!

I kicked him.

He strapped weights to my ankles.

This time I didn't ask him if he was sure.

I punched him.

He ducked.

I tried again.

He sidestepped.

I tried again …

It was like trying to hit a
mosquito with a baseball bat.

71

He gave me a piece of string ... and told me what to do.

You're quicker already!

Yup – I'd be just fine if I was entering a string-snatching competition with Fluffy ...

But I'm not – I'm fighting Hulk in a taekwondo competition!!!

Spot wanted to help too.

Eric decided I should race Spot to get quicker.

Spot beat me every time.

In the last race, he sat down and waited for me.

It looks like I won't even be able to outrun Hulk ...

Even an oak tree was a seed once...

Yes, and so were a string bean and a sunflower!
Not to mention a weed!!

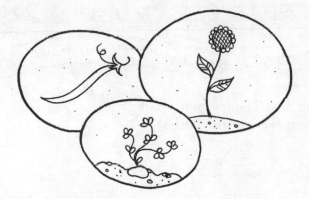

At school the next day ...

Only two days to go, dweeb!

Just you and me and a small square mat. Nowhere to run and nowhere to hide.

CHAPTER 13 | Never show fear.

I'm looking forward to it.

Remember, if you don't last three rounds – the deal is off.

Yep. I'm looking forward to it - like a trip to the dentist ...

Or going cage-diving with sharks ...

Or wrestling a grizzly bear.

When I got home, Spot and Fluffy were waiting for me. So was a long black snake.

No, it was my belt. Someone had coloured it black with a texta.

I was so desperate, I read Dad's book ...

I guess that's because whoever came in second is DEAD!

I asked Master Choi for advice ...

Suppose I was to fight someone larger and stronger and better, Master Choi - how would I ... errr, win?

To win one must combine the rage of a tiger, the speed of a dragon, the courage of a bear and the cunning of a snake.

Oh! That's easy, then. I'll get right on it. NOT.

Or maybe I'll try the rage of a rabbit, the speed of a sloth, the courage of a pigeon and the cunning of a mule?

The day of the fight.

I put on my armour. I put on my black belt.

I hugged Spot and Fluffy and then hid them in my bag.

Even though it was a secret, everyone seemed to know about the taekwondo competition.

Break a leg, Marcus!

I probably will ...

Chin up, Marcus!

That will just give Hulk one more thing to hit ...

Hulk was waiting ...

ROUND 1

The bell rang …

I figured out what to do – I needed to waste time.
The more time I wasted, the less time he had to hurt me.

Hulk came closer.

I collapsed to the ground and clutched my ankle.

Hulk got a point! He didn't even touch me!

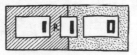

You're not allowed to fake an injury.

I'm not faking an injury –

– I'm anticipating it …

Hulk rushed at me ...

I turned and ran. He chased me!
I ran out of the area!!

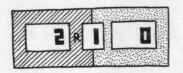

Hulk got a point!!!

You're hot allowed to step out of the area!

Hulk aimed a punch at my chest.

I jumped back.
I tripped over my feet.

Hulk got a point!

What??

I just fell over!

You're not allowed to fall over on purpose!

It was an accident!!

Hulk was mad now.

He rushed at me, grabbed my uniform and shoved me. I ended up outside the area again. Great – another point for Hulk.

ROUND 2

So far, so good.

One round done and I wasn't even injured. And I was only one point behind.

Hulk attacked!

Don't count my chickens?
How about the birds?

He hit me seven times.

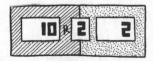

Hulk held up three fingers.

I knew what he meant. I had to last three rounds. Or Fluffy would never get back to JT.

I saw JT waving at me. I knew I had to stay in.

ROUND 3

Hulk and I faced each other.

It was Lizzie, my friend
from soccer – still
wearing her Liverpool kit.

I imagined the ball ...

I got a point!
I got a point!!
I got a point!!!

(Pity I missed his head – that would have been
three points.)

Hulk was mad now. He charged at me ...

Remember the sidestep, Marcus!

It was Tank from rugby!
I sidestepped.
Hulk was going so fast,
he ran out of the area.

10 R 3   4

Now try a
drop kick!

I did!

10 R 3   5

Hulk tried again.

It was the Little Master,
my friend from cricket.
I knew just what he meant.

I blocked three kicks in a row.

Hulk was so angry, he kicked me in the knee.

He punched
me in the head.

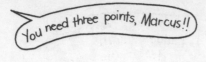 You need three points, Marcus!!

Three points? How in the world was I going to do that?

I spotted Lizzie. She had a ball under her arm. She threw it in the air and volleyed it against the back wall.

Good idea!

Great roundhouse kick, Marcus!

10 × 3 10

This time I hit his head!!! Three points!!!

A draw! And I'm still standing!

And JT will get Fluffy back!

RRIIIINNNGGGGG!!

90

Phew! They need to change their expressions.

It was Dad and Master Choi.

How did they find out about the fight?

I told him about Hulk, JT and Fluffy.

I realised something important. I had to finish
the fight.
It was the only way to deal with bullies.
Show them you weren't afraid.

Unless, of course, you had
a chance to rescue
their kitten instead.

So that wasn't
going to work.

I spotted Fluffy
and Spot ... and had an idea!

SUDDEN DEATH ROUND

I pulled a thread from my uniform
and clutched it in my fists.

Hulk charged at me.

I evaded him with my
personal poomsae.

Master Choi looked
depressed.

Dad looked embarrassed.

Everyone else just looked.

Including Hulk.

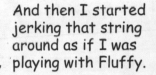

And then I started jerking that string around as if I was playing with Fluffy.

My fists were like lightning bolts.

I punched Hulk in the chest using the Hammer Fist!

He swung his leg out ...
I remembered Spot jumping up to lick my face.
I leapt in the air!

Dad says I can keep Fluffy because I didn't get into any fights.
Great!
Hey, Marcus!
What?
Thanks.
Purrrrrrrr!
I guess these fights will be easier once I get my other belts, Dad!
Other belts?
No way!
I'm not letting you do anything that dangerous again!
From now on – you just do stuff where you get to stay away from the other competitors!!!
The way you leapt in the air...
You were born to jump! I just know it!

About the Author

Shamini Flint lives in Singapore with her husband and two children. She is an ex-lawyer, ex-lecturer, stay-at-home mum and writer. She loves taekwondo!

www.shaminiflint.com

Have you read my Rugby Diary?

What about my Cricket Diary?

And of course
my Soccer Diary!

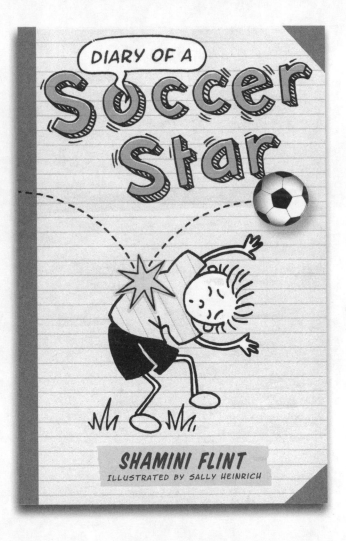